¡Así debemos ser!
Way to Be!

Preocuparse por los demás
Caring

por/by Mary Small   ilustrado por/illustrated by Stacey Previn

Gracias a nuestros asesores por su experiencia, investigación y asesoría/
Thanks to our advisers for their expertise, research, and advice:

Bambi L. Wagner, Directora de Educación/Director of Education
Instituto para el Desarrollo del Carácter/Institute for Character Development, Des Moines, Iowa
Miembro y Capacitadora de la Docencia Nacional/National Faculty Member and Trainer
Instituto Josephson de Ética/Josephson Institute of Ethics - CHARACTER COUNTS!sm
Los Angeles, California

Susan Kesselring, Educadora de Alfabetismo/M.A., Literacy Educator
Distrito Escolar Rosemount-Apple Valley-Eagan (Minnesota)/
Rosemount-Apple Valley-Eagan (Minnesota) School District

PICTURE WINDOW BOOKS
a capstone imprint

Editor: Jacqueline A. Wolfe
Translation Services: Strictly Spanish
Designer: Eric Manske
Production Specialist: Sarah Bennett
Art Director: Nathan Gassman
Managing Editor: Catherine Neitge
The illustrations in this book were created with acrylics.

Picture Window Books
151 Good Counsel Drive
P.O. Box 669
Mankato, MN 56002-0669
877-845-8392
www.capstonepub.com

All books published by Picture Window Books are manufactured with paper containing at least 10 percent post-consumer waste.

Library of Congress Cataloging-in-Publication Data
Small, Mary.
  [Caring. Spanish & English]
  Preocuparse por los demás / por Mary Small ; ilustrado por Stacey Previn = Caring / by
Mary Small ; illustrated by Stacey Previn.
  p. cm.—(¡Así debemos ser! = Way to be!)
Summary: "Explains many different ways that children can show they care—in both English and
Spanish"—Provided by publisher.
  Includes index.
  ISBN 978-1-4048-6692-8 (library binding)
  1. Caring—Juvenile literature. I. Previn, Stacey. II. Title: Caring. III. Series.
BJ1475.S6218 2011
177'.7—dc22
                                                                    2010040921

Printed in the United States of America in North Mankato, Minnesota.
092010   005933CGS11

When you care about people,

it matters to you what happens to them. You want them to be safe and happy. When they are sad or angry or frightened, you want to help.

You can care about your family, your friends, people who live in your neighborhood—even your pets.

There are lots of ways to show you care.

Cuando te preocupas por las personas,

te importa lo que les sucede. Quieres que estén seguros y sean felices. Cuando están tristes o enojados o asustados, quieres ayudar.

Tú te puedes preocupar por tu familia, tus amigos, las personas que viven en tu vecindario, incluso tus mascotas.

Hay muchas formas de demostrar que te preocupas por los demás.

Bill offers to share his sucker with his older sister.

He is showing her he cares.

Bill ofrece compartir su golosina con su hermana mayor.

Él le está demostrando que se preocupa por ella.

Even though sometimes it's hard, Aaron keeps a close eye on his brother and sister.

He is showing them he cares.

Aunque a veces es difícil, Aaron cuida atentamente a su hermano y a su hermana.

Él les está demostrando que se preocupa por ellos.

On special days, Caroline makes sure everyone feels included.

She is showing she cares.

En días especiales, Caroline se asegura que todos se sientan incluidos.

Ella está demostrando que se preocupa por los demás.

Joshua always holds the door open to let other people go in first.

He is showing he cares.

Joshua siempre sostiene la puerta para que otras personas entren primero.

Él está demostrando que se preocupa por los demás.

Tim stops his friends from fighting and helps them to make up.

He is showing he cares.

Tim evita que sus amigos
se peleen y los ayuda
a reconciliarse.

Él está demostrando que se
preocupa por los demás.

Nathan lets his best friend play with his favorite toy.

He is showing he cares.

───────────────

Nathan deja que su mejor amigo juegue con su juguete favorito.

Él está demostrando que se preocupa por los demás.

Freddie helps his dad work on the family car.

He is showing he cares.

———————

Freddie ayuda a su papá a trabajar en el auto de la familia.

Él está demostrando que se preocupa por los demás.

Emily and Krista ask the new boy in school to sit with them during lunch.

They are showing they care.

———————————————

Emily y Krista invitan al nuevo niño de la escuela a sentarse con ellas durante el almuerzo.

Ellas están demostrando que se preocupan por los demás.

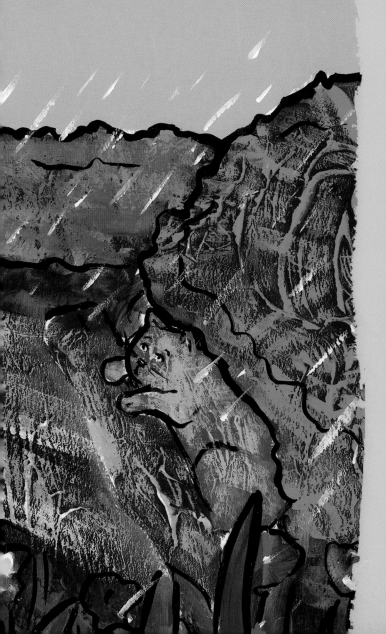

Ashley goes out during a rainstorm to help find her lost cat.

She is showing she cares.

Ashley sale durante una tormenta de lluvia para ayudar a encontrar a su gato perdido.

Ella está demostrando que se preocupa por los demás.

Mark and Alice share their favorite book.

They are showing each other they care.

Mark y Alice comparten su libro favorito.

Ellos están demostrando que se preocupan uno por el otro.

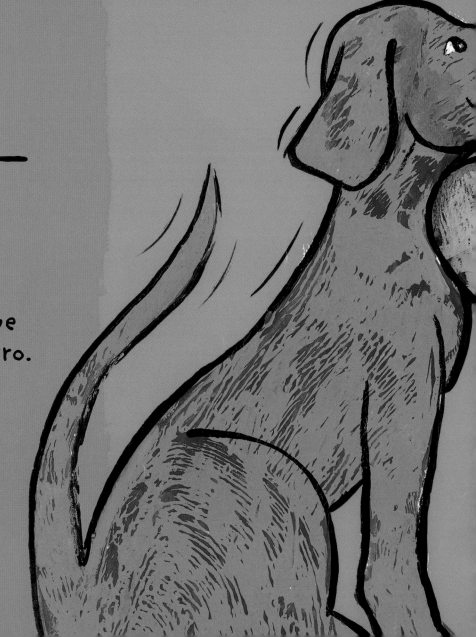

Internet Sites

FactHound offers a safe, fun way to find Internet sites related to this book.
All of the sites on FactHound have been researched by our staff.

Here's all you do:

Visit www.facthound.com

Type in this code: 9781404866928

Index

Super-cool stuff!

Check out projects, games and lots more at www.capstonekids.com

---

Sitios de Internet

FactHound brinda una forma segura y divertida de encontrar sitios de Internet relacionados con este libro. Todos los sitios en FactHound han sido investigados por nuestro personal.

Esto es todo lo que tienes que hacer:

Visita www.facthound.com

Ingresa este código: 9781404866928

Índice

¡Algo súper divertido!

Hay proyectos, juegos y mucho más en www.capstonekids.com

Canadian Families

CANADIANS AT SCHOOL

TRUE NORTH

BY SHERI DOYLE

True North is published by Beech Street Books
27 Stewart Rd. Collingwood, ON Canada L9Y 4M7

www.beechstreetbooks.ca

Produced by Red Line Editorial

Photographs ©: Digital Vision/Photodisc/Thinkstock, cover, 1; Purestock/Thinkstock, 4–5; Red Line Editorial, 6; James Boardman/Hemera/Thinkstock, 8–9; Craig E. Divine/Shutterstock Images, 10–11; wckiw/iStockphoto, 12–13; margouillatphotos/iStockphoto, 14–15; Bill Brooks/Alamy, 16–17; Lee Brown/Alamy, 18–19; BananaStock/Thinkstock, 20–21

Editor: Heather C. Hudak
Designer: Laura Polzin

Library and Archives Canada Cataloguing in Publication

Doyle, Sheri, author
       Canadians at school / by Sheri Doyle.

(Canadian families)
Includes bibliographical references and index.
Issued in print and electronic formats.
ISBN 978-1-77308-010-9 (hardback).--ISBN 978-1-77308-038-3 (paperback).--ISBN 978-1-77308-066-6 (pdf).--ISBN 978-1-77308-094-9 (html)

       1. Education, Elementary--Canada--Juvenile literature.
2. Elementary schools--Canada--Juvenile literature. 3. Students--Canada--Juvenile literature. I. Title.

LB1556.7.C3D69 2016   j372.971   C2016-903176-4
                                           C2016-903177-2

Printed in the United States of America
Mankato, MN
August 2016

TABLE OF CONTENTS

Chapter One

IN THE CLASSROOM

Kids all across Canada go to school. Some students walk to school. Other students take a bus or get a ride. The school day starts in the early morning.

Students begin their day by singing "O Canada." Many students sing the words in English or French. Some students sing the song in other languages, such as those belonging to aboriginal communities.

Canadian students learn to read books. They write stories and **poems**. They write down facts for projects. Some students write in English. Other students write in French.

Three million Canadian kids take a school bus each day.

4

FAST FACT

Some students are new to Canada. They moved to Canada from other countries, such as Guyana, India, and China. These students may need to learn English for the first time. Many students speak other languages at home. These include Hindi, Polish, and Vietnamese. Some students' families have lived in Canada for a long time.

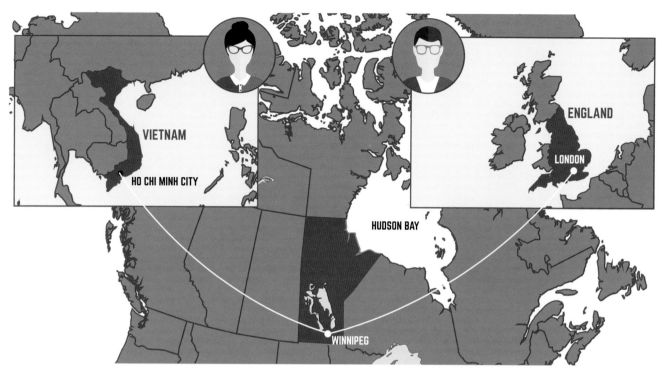

THE KENT-NGUYEN FAMILY

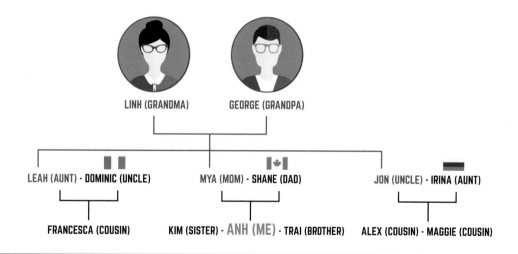

LINH (GRANDMA)   GEORGE (GRANDPA)

LEAH (AUNT) - DOMINIC (UNCLE)   MYA (MOM) - SHANE (DAD)   JON (UNCLE) - IRINA (AUNT)

FRANCESCA (COUSIN)   KIM (SISTER) - ANH (ME) - TRAI (BROTHER)   ALEX (COUSIN) - MAGGIE (COUSIN)

George and Linh both came to Canada from other countries. They met in Winnipeg and got married. This is their family.

6

Students learn about their community. They also learn about the people who live in it. They learn how their family is a part of the community. Students find out about people who work in their community. They learn about doctors, teachers, and bakers.

Students also learn math skills. They work on math problems using numbers, pictures, and words. In science, students learn about animals. They also learn about water and air. They do experiments. They write down the results in a chart. They make **conclusions**.

Chapter Two

TIME TO MOVE

Recess is a break from the classroom. Moving around and playing with friends is healthy for the body and mind. Kids play outside on the playground or in the field. Some kids play sports like soccer or basketball. Others play with skipping ropes or on the **monkey bars**. Many kids play tag.

Gym class helps students stay fit. Students do warm-ups before playing sports. They stretch on mats. They jog around the gym or field. Then they play a sport, such as floor hockey or lacrosse.

Lacrosse is the national summer sport of Canada.

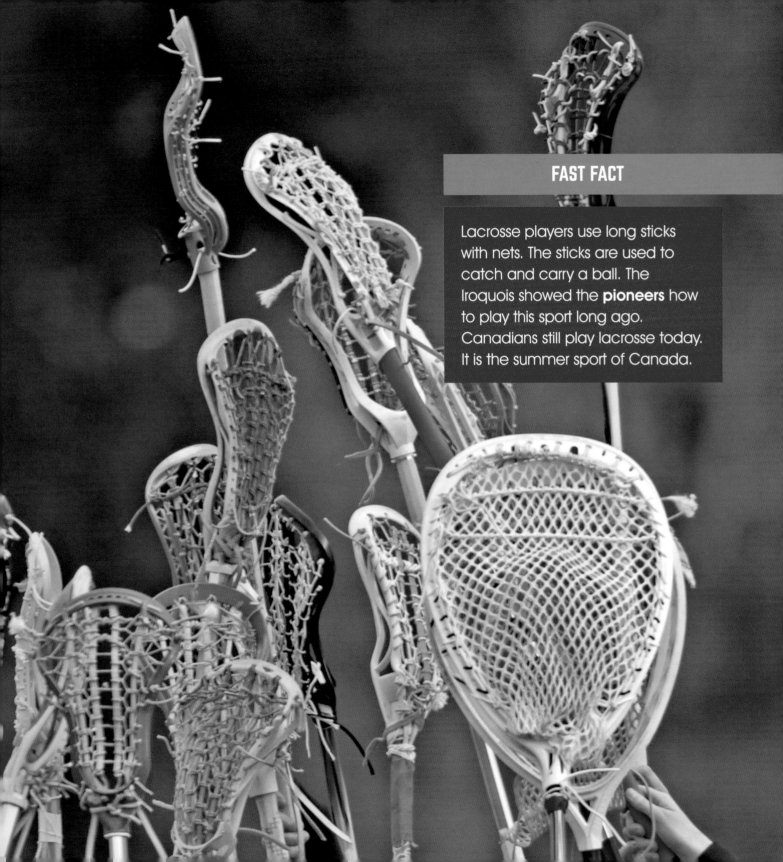

Chapter Three

TAKING PART IN THE ARTS

Students learn to play music from around the world. They sing songs. They also play instruments. Some students learn to play steel drums. The steel drums are from Jamaica.

Students learn dances at school. Some students learn a **Cree** hoop dance. They use many small hoops to tell a story as they move. Kids dance to the beat of a big drum. Some students learn Scottish dancing. They step, skip, and hop. They dance to the sound of bagpipes.

Students work on class plays. Plays are one way to tell a story. Some kids act in plays for Black History Month. They learn about important people and events.

Some kids learn to play instruments in school.

10

Some Canadians play bagpipes. The player blows into a pipe. The air goes into the bag. Then the air moves from the bag to other parts to make sounds. Bagpipes are from Scotland.

Every student gets a part in a class play. Some are actors. Others build sets. Plays are often performed on a stage. Some take place in the school gym.

Black History Month takes place in February each year. Students make posters, read books, and make crafts. They learn about how black Canadians helped shape Canada.

Students learn many skills in art class. They may learn how to make **Inuit** art. They carve polar bears out of soapstone. Students draw Canadian animals, such as **Arctic** foxes. They paint pictures of the land. Some paint maple leaves. Others paint the Arctic sky with many colours, just like the Northern Lights.

Origami is the Japanese art of folding paper into shapes.

INQUIRY QUESTIONS ?

When did your classmates' families come to Canada? Where did they come from?

Chapter Four

TIME FOR LUNCH

Students are hungry by lunchtime. Food helps the body grow and stay healthy.

Some foods are better for the body than other foods. Sugary or very salty food is not good for the body. Fresh food is best! *Canada's Food Guide* lists the best foods for health. It helps kids make healthy choices.

Canadians take many kinds of foods for lunch. Some students eat cold food. This may be cheese, yogurt, or **mango** chunks. Other kids have hot food, such as pasta and meatballs. Many kids bring leftovers. They may have chicken **curry** or noodles.

Many kids take sandwiches to school for lunch.

Chapter Five

ON THE ROAD

Sometimes students go on field trips. They may go to skating rinks and swimming pools. Some kids go to plays and visit farms. They meet new people on trips. They meet actors, farmers, and athletes.

Many Canadian students visit maple syrup farms in March. Students see **sap** drip from a hole in a tree trunk. The sap drips into a bucket. Later, sap is boiled until it becomes syrup. The syrup tastes very sweet!

A class party can be a lot of fun. Students bring food from home. They decorate the classroom. They listen to music and play games. Sometimes kids dress up in costumes.

Kids enjoy maple taffy at a festival in Ontario.

Schools celebrate important events, such as Terry Fox Day. In 1980, Terry Fox began to run across Canada to raise money to fight **cancer**. Kids today still take part in Terry Fox Day. Students and teachers go for a walk or jog together.

Remembrance Day is on November 11 each year. Students take time to remember those who still serve, served, or lost their lives in wars. Everyone takes a minute to be silent. Students sing songs. They read poems, such as "In Flanders Fields."

Kids who take part in Terry Fox Runs raise money to fund cancer research.

Chapter Six

JOIN THE CLUB

Many students take part in school clubs. Some kids play sports like soccer, volleyball, or hockey. Others join clubs.

Clubs give students the chance to learn about each other and the world around them. Kids may take part in French, craft, or library clubs. Some students are part of a homework club. They can get help from other students and teachers.

Some students go to **choir**. They learn songs from other parts of the world, such as Germany or Iran. Students often learn new words.

More than twice as many kids under the age of 14 play soccer than hockey in Canada.

GLOSSARY

ARCTIC
the cold northern parts of Canada

CANCER
a type of disease that involves abnormal cell growth

CHOIR
a group of people who sing together

CONCLUSIONS
final decisions or judgments

CREE
a First Nations group that has its own unique culture and traditions

CURRY
an Indian spice blend

INUIT
relating to the people and places of northern Canada and parts of Alaska and Greenland

MANGO
a fruit that grows in Asia and other warm places

MONKEY BARS
playground equipment with bars to hang from

PIONEERS
settlers who came to Canada from Europe long ago

POEMS
types of writing that use parts of speech and song

SAP
a liquid that comes from trees and plants

TO LEARN MORE

BOOKS

Friesen, Helen Lepp. *Maple Syrup*. Calgary: Weigl Educational Publishers, 2012.

Kalman, Bobbie. *Canada: The People*. St. Catharines, ON: Crabtree Publishing, 2010.

Macleod, Elizabeth and Frieda Wishinsky. *Colossal Canada: 100 Epic Facts and Feasts*. Toronto: Scholastic Canada Ltd., 2015.

WEBSITES

CANADIAN GEOGRAPHIC KIDS!
www.canadiangeographic.ca/kids/default.asp

KIDS' STOP: INDIGENOUS AND NORTHERN AFFAIRS CANADA
www.aadnc-aandc.gc.ca/eng/1302889494709/1302889781786

NATIONAL GEOGRAPHIC KIDS
kids.nationalgeographic.com/explore/countries/canada/#canada-playing-hockey.jpg

INDEX

ABOUT THE AUTHOR

Sheri Doyle is an author of books, articles, and poems for children and adults.